"Tiger, will you watch Cub?

He'll be as good as gold. 'Bye!"

by Jonny Lambert

Tiger Tiger

"Ummm . . . ."

tiger tales

Cub stared at Tiger.

Tiger frowned at Cub.

Slump! Flump!

"Ugh!" sighed Tiger.

"I'm too old for cub-sitting.

"Now stay there, Cub, and don't move."

Huff! Puff! Pout!

Cub grew bored as Tiger snored.

"Tiger, Tiger, don't sleep all day.

Get up! Wake up! I want to play!"

"Play?" grumbled Tiger. "At my age?

I suppose we could go for a very slow walk."

Dart! Dash! Rush!

Cub ran along the jungle trail.

Tiger followed, nose to tail.

"Tiger, Tiger, come on! Let's run!

I want to explore. I want to have FUN!"

"Grrrr," growled Tiger. "It's too hot to explore. And there's nothing to see around here anymore."

Flit! Float! Flutter!

The butterfly gleamed, and Cub beamed.

"Tiger, Tiger, look what I found.

Down here! SEE? On the ground!"

"Nonsense," muttered Tiger. "That's just a grub.
It's time to go back and take a nap now, Cub."

Chitter-chatter! Screech!
Monkeys swung to and fro.
  "But Tiger, Tiger, there's more to see!
Look up! Way up! High up in the tree!"

"I see them," mumbled Tiger.
"I remember that noisy bunch!"

Bristle! Sniff! Twitch!

"Cub, Cub, don't make a sound!"

Tiger snarled and stood his ground.

Crawl! Creep! Crouch!
"Stay close to me," Tiger whispered,
moving quietly.

Snort! Stomp!
Crashing through, two tiny rhinos
dashed into view.

"Gosh!" Tiger exclaimed. "Baby rhinos!
How rare! Look, Cub . . . ."

Tiger turned, but Cub wasn't there!

Clasp! Claw! Clamber!
Cub excitedly climbed up the
nearest tree.

"Tiger, Tiger, look! Who is this?
Above me."

"Oh, my!" smiled Tiger. "You've found Pangolin. But Cub, Cub, come back down. Here, where it's safe. On the ground!"

Cling! Grip! Grasp!

Cub held on tight, squeaking with delight.

"NO! I WON'T! You can't catch me . . . .

I'm just too quick! Look and see!"

Spring! Jump! Catch!

"Aha!" laughed Tiger. "Not quite quick enough!
That was so much FUN. Now get ready, Cub, and
watch these Sambar deer . . ."

"...RUN!"

Startled by the stripy old cat, the grazing
deer scattered this way and that.

Leap! Laugh! Giggle!
Bouncing along the jungle trail,
Tiger chased Cub, nose to tail.

"Tiger, Tiger, can we explore some more?"

Cub didn't want the day to end.

Tiger smiled. "Of course we can . . ."

"...my little friend."